Aqualicious

WRITTEN AND ILLUSTRATED BY

Victoria Kann

HARPER

An Imprint of HarperCollinsPublishers

Library of Congress Cataloging-in-Publication Data
Kann, Victoria, author, illustrator.
 Aqualicious / written and illustrated by Victoria Kann. — First edition.
  pages cm. — (Pinkalicious)
 Summary: At the beach, Pinkalicious and her brother help a tiny mermaid, a merminnie, to go back
home.
 ISBN 978-0-06-233016-1 (trade bdg.) — ISBN 978-0-06-233017-8 (lib. bdg.) — ISBN 978-0-06-239733-1 (int'l ed.)
 [1. Mermaids—Fiction. 2. Beaches—Fiction. 3. Brothers and sisters—Fiction.] I. Title.
 PZ7.K12774Aqu 2015
 [E]—dc23
2014005861
CIP
AC

The artist used mixed media to create the digital illustrations for this book.
Typography by Rachel Zegar
20 21 SCP 10 9
❖
First Edition

I was collecting seashells. I found a shell and held it next to my ear so I could listen to the ocean.

Instead of hearing the ocean, I heard a little voice inside the shell.

"Put me down! I'm trying to nap!" the voice said.

"Eeeek!" I screamed. I was scared, but I was also curious. I looked inside the shell. I saw a little face with long hair.

"Can you help me?" said the little voice.

"Help you? What are you?" I asked.

"I am Aqua," she said shyly, wiggling out of the shell.

"Hi! My name is Pinkalicious," I said.

"Oh, I love the color pink, but blue is my favorite color," Aqua said. "I am a merminnie."

"What is a merminnie?" I asked.

"Merminnies are a smaller, rarer species of mermaids," said Aqua. "Just like there are lots of different kinds of fish, there are many different kinds of mermaids. Merminnies only inhabit this sea coast. I am actually quite well known, and I . . ."

"WOWEEE!" I screamed excitedly before she could finish. "I didn't think mermaids or merminnies actually existed!"

I put Aqua in my bucket so I could show her to my brother, Peter.

"Peter, look what I found—a merminnie mermaid!" I said. Peter
was burying Mommy and Daddy in the sand while they napped.
I dumped the contents of the bucket onto the towel.
"Say something, Aqua," I commanded.

"I was actually speaking to you when you put me in your pail of periwinkles, hermit crabs, and seashells, which I do not appreciate—hermit crabs bite! I'd like to go home now, please."

"YES! You do need a home!" Peter said. "Come on, Pinkalicious, let's build a palace for her. I bet she is a princess!"

Peter and I immediately got to work. We built a big sand castle with turrets and decorated it with shells, stones, and feathers.

"Do you like it, Aqua?" I asked.

"Yes, I do like it. It is lovely, but it isn't my home. I live underwater and I should get back there," she said.

"Of course! But wouldn't you like to have lunch with us first?" asked Peter.

"Hmm, what are you eating? Normally I only eat algae and phytoplankton. Human food would be a real treat!" she said.

I put Aqua in my water cup and carried her to the concession stand to let her pick out her lunch.

"I would like one of EVERYTHING!" she said. "And don't forget the sea salt!"

"Would you like to play miniature golf with us?" I asked Aqua after lunch.

"All you have to do is hit the little ball into the hole," Peter said.

"I'll help you, but then I really should be going," Aqua said as she hid in the hole on the putting green.

"Just hit the ball and I will grab it, and then you will win!"
"That's cheating! I don't want to play if you can't play fairly,"
I said, stomping back to the beach.

"Sorry, Pinkalicious," Aqua said. "Perhaps I can teach you to surf? Just balance on this board and ride through the waves like this!"

"Wheeeeeee, this is funtastic!" I said.

"Uh-oh, Pinkalicious. That looks dangerous. I am going to wake up Mommy and Daddy if you are going to stay in the water," said Peter from the shore.

Suddenly a seagull grabbed Aqua and flew away.
"HELP, help me! PLEASE! Don't let it eat me!" Aqua screamed
as she dangled from its beak.

"Quick, Peter, the gull is by the lighthouse! We can still save Aqua!" I said, running as fast as I could.

"Hurry! Before she becomes merminnie mincemeat!" said Peter.

"Don't worry, Aqua!" Peter threw a mussel to the seagull, who dropped Aqua into the soft sea grass. Peter picked her up from the ground. We quickly climbed into a little sailboat before the seagull came back for her.

"You'll be safe here. We will protect you," said Peter.

"Thank you for saving me! I really appreciate it, but now it's time for me to go home. You humans lead such exhausting lives," sighed Aqua.

"Okay, Aqua, you can go back home," Peter said as he carefully put Aqua in the water.

"So long, Aqua, it was nice to meet you!" I said, waving good-bye.

"What are you doing?" screamed Aqua. "NOOOOOO! Help me! There are sharks and eels and horrible crabs in there. This is not my home! Get me out of here!"

Peter scooped Aqua out of the water and brought her back to our towel.

"If you don't live in the sea, where do you live?" I asked.

"Over there," said Daddy, who was now awake and pointing to a building on the other side of the sand dune.

"Aqua is famous! We came to this beach so we could visit the aquarium where Aqua lives. She is a real merminnie. We were going to tell you all about her but I guess we fell asleep," said Mommy.

"Sometimes I like to sneak out to go to the beach and see what I can discover. It's good to be curious. You never know what you will find. And you humans are lots of fun! Now I need to get back home to my tank before anyone notices that I am gone. Will you take me?" asked Aqua.

Inside the aquarium Aqua swam in her tank. There was a crowd of people who clapped and cheered for her. She was famous! As she swam by on her seahorse, she waved to us.

I whispered, "Thank you, Aqua. You are blue-tiful!"

Afterward we got blueberry and sea swirl ice cream.
"Today was truly Aqualicious!" I said. "Who knew that
collecting seashells could be so much fun?"